T0128596

A Poster From My Grandfather

LYNETTE ALLI

Illustrated By Gail Jacalan

To order additional copies of this book, contact:
Xlibris
844-714-8691
www.Xlibris.com
Orders@Xlibris.com

ISBN: Softcover   978-1-6698-4107-4
        Hardcover   978-1-6698-4108-1
        EBook   978-1-6698-4109-8

Print information available on the last page

Rev. date: 03/07/2023

NICE WORDS MAKE LIFE HAPPY,

AND SUCCESSFUL.

LOVE AND OBEY YOUR PARENTS, TREAT THEM, AND EVERYONE WITH RESPECT.

OBEY THE LAWS OF YOUR COUNTRY.

HELP OTHERS IF, AND WHEN YOU CAN.

LISTEN TO WHAT OTHERS HAVE TO SAY.

WE LEARN FROM EACH OTHER.

ALWAYS SPEAK THE TRUTH.

DO NOT BULLY OTHERS, AND DO NOT TAKE THINGS THAT ARE NOT YOURS.

EVERYONE MAKE MISTAKES, AND MISTAKES CAN BE CORRECTED.

BE KIND TO PEOPLE AND ANIMALS.

ALWAYS BEHAVE YOUR BEST AND TAKE YOUR SCHOOL LESSONS SERIOUSLY.

REMEMBER TO SMILE, HAVE A GOOD LAUGH AND BE POLITE.

LOVE   GRANDFATHER.

NICE WORDS ARE MAGICAL

PLEASE, THANK YOU, SORRY, EXCUSE ME.

FOR LEA.

FROM GRANDFATHER WITH LOV

My name is Lia, I started my early life with a

beautiful POSTER from my grandfather.

This is my story about my POSTER, with magical words.

I was in kindergarten when I got my POSTER. I did not know to read or write.

I am now six years old, I am in elementary school, I can read, and write.

It was the end of summer holidays; I was excited to return to school.

I planned to get my new books ready, to start my new class.

While I was putting my new books in my new pink

backpack, I noticed my POSTER in our bookcase.

I remembered my POSTER and I took it out.

I looked at it again and again, then I read the

words and sentences again and again.

Now I understand the words and sentences on my Poster.

I showed my parents my POSTER and they told
me how and when I got my POSTER.
My mom and dad told me this part of my POSTER story.
On a bright sunny day in August, three years ago, our families
celebrated our grandfather's sixty fifth birthday.
It was at a family picnic in, 'Happy Acres Park'.
At the picnic everyone had, hot dogs, hamburgers, drink, fruits, and ice cream.
We sang happy birthday songs to grandfather, he blew the candles from
his cake and thanked everyone for making his birthday special.
All the adults chatted and played games with the children.

Everyone was getting ready to go home, when, our grandfather
said, "I have a gift for all my grandchildren."
He then gave me, my sister Ella, my brother Kevin and
all my cousins a POSTER and a bag of candies.
We were delighted and thanked our grandfather.
I was sitting on grandma's lap when I got my POSTER.
My parents told me I held on to my POSTER and
did not want anyone to touch it.

FOR ALL MY GRANDCHILDREN.
HERE IS A MAP TO FOLLOW:

NICE WORDS MAKE LIFE HAPPY.
    AND SUCCESSFUL ..
LOVE AND OBEY YOUR PARENTS, TREAT THEM, AND
EVERYONE WITH RESPECT.
OBEY THE LAWS OF YOUR COUNTRY.
HELP OTHERS IF, AND WHEN YOU CAN.
LISTEN TO WHAT OTHERS HAVE TO SAY.
WE LEARN FROM EACH OTHER.

ALWAYS SPEAK THE TRUTH.
DO NOT BULLY OTHERS, AND DO NOT TAKE THINGS THAT
ARE NOT YOURS.
EVERYONE MAKE MISTAKES, AND MISTAKE CAN BE

NIMALS.
EST AND TAKE YOUR SCHOOL

Now I know how and when I got my POSTER.

I looked again at my POSTER and read the words and sentences.

Then I wrote some words and sentences on my POSTER.

This is what I wrote.

My Life LESSONS.

This POSTER is my precious gift, and it is my guide to follow.

This will make me an honest loveable child and a respectful person.

The paper will get old and torn but the words will always be remembered.

Lea, Thanks grandpa.

As soon as I finished writing words on my Poster,
Ella and Kevin came into our study room.
They told me, we would be going in the morning to
have breakfast with our grandparents.
I showed Ella and Kevin my POSTER with the new words.
I said to them, "This is my POSTER, with words and
sentences I wrote on it, do you like my new
POSTER?"
My brother and sister told me they loved the new words and
sentences, and they were impressed with my work.

I said to Ella and Kevin, "tell me about your POSTERS."
Ella said, "Three years ago, I used my POSTER as a school
project, my teacher read the words and sentences to my class,
everyone told me that I have great grandparents.
My POSTER is with my prized possessions."
Kevin then answered, "mom and dad promised to frame
my POSTER for my next birthday, its precious and my
framed POSTER will be in my room for always."

Ella and Kevin told me to take my POSTER to show our grandparents, I
was excited, and I will take my POSTER to show our grandparents.
I said to Ella and Kevin, "Our POSTERS are our family treasures."
They nodded in agreement.

The next morning, my sister Ella, my brother Kevin, my parents,
and I were going to have breakfast with out grandparents.
I loved to visit our grandparents but today I am overjoyed, because I
will show them my POSTER with the new words and sentences.
I told my parents about my POSTER but they will
have to wait to see it with our grandparents.
My parents told me they are looking forward to seeing
the new words and sentences on my POSTER.

We greeted our grandparents and then had a delicious breakfast with them.

While we were having breakfast, I said to our grandparents, "grandma

and grandpa, I have a family treasure, I will show you after breakfast."

They were looking at my pink backpack, they told me

they can not wait to see the family treasure.

After breakfast, we went and sat in our grandparents' family room.

I showed my parents and grandparents my POSTER, with
the new words and sentences, and I asked them, "do you
like my POSTER, with new words and sentences?"
Everyone was quiet for a few minutes, then our grandfather said, "Lea,
you are a brave child, I really like the added words and sentences.
I know all my grandchildren will remember to read
and follow the words on their POSTERS."
Lea, replied," not to worry grandpa, I will talk to all my cousins and make sure
they understand the importance of the words and sentences on their POSTERS."
Lea's mom, grandpa and grandma clapped their hands.
Lea's dad smiled, he was very happy with the words, Lea wrote on her Poster.

My sister, brother, and I, thanked our grandma for giving us
presents, goodies, for babysitting us, and for wiping our tears.
We then thanked our grandpa for reciting poems,
singing songs, and telling us stories.
Our grandparents told us, all their grandchildren,
are nice, obedient, loving, and courteous.

I said to my grandfather, "grandpa, I know the stories you
told us, the songs you sang for us and the poems you
recited for us, are all about life lessons on the Poster.
My grandfather replied, "Lea, you are my youngest grandchild,
and yes, the POSTER have life lessons and yes, they are taken from
stories, poems, and songs, I shared with all my grandchildren.
The POSTER is a map with nice words, which will lead
to an honest, respectful, and successful life.
ALL CHILDREN ARE BEAUTIFUL."
Lia, replied, "just like my parents, my grandparents, other
parents and grandparents, are all role models."

We had a great morning; we said our goodbyes and went home.

That night, I imagined, when I was a little girl, now I am a

big girl, next I will be a mother and grandmother.

I said to myself, "I will read the words and sentences on

my POSTER, often to remember the life lessons.

The life lessons will make me, an honest, wise, happy and

law -abiding citizen, like our parents and grandparents.

I will also give my grandchildren a POSTER with nice words."

I was sleepy and slept until morning.

That is the end of my POSTER STORY.LOVE TO ALL.

Printed in the United States
by Baker & Taylor Publisher Services